WILD LOVE

Sapphic Mountain, Book One

Gemma Addison Dove

CONTENTS

About the Book

Cupcake baker Nelly needs to make it to her sister's cabin for her birthday, but grumpy mountain woman Lora is the only one available to drive her. When a storm causes a tree to fall and block their path, they're forced to take shelter in Lora's cozy cabin. And there's only one bed.

Wild Love is a steamy sapphic instalove short romance featuring a thirty-two-year-old mountain woman falling for the sweetest girl in town.

This quick read includes:

- Sapphic romance/women loving women.

- Pansexual main character.

- Lesbian main character.

- Grumpy/Sunshine.

- Age gap romance (22/32).

- Best friend's little sister/Older sister's best friend.

- A cozy cabin with only one bed.

- V-card.

- Teach me vibes.

- Beater licking.

- Steamy scenes.

- Consent is sexy.

- Dual POV.

- Happily Ever After ending.

- And cupcakes.

A Note from the Author

This is a work of fiction. All characters are over eighteen and are consenting adults. There are no family relations between characters. This is a steamy sapphic romance with mature themes and is intended for readers eighteen or older. No AI was used to assist in writing this story, and no AI was used by the cover designer for this book.

CHAPTER ONE: NELLY

I look down at my list, taking stock of all my supplies: flour, sugar, baking soda, baking powder, vanilla, icing sugar, and my sister Samantha should have fresh eggs from her chicken coop, and some milk and butter. That should be everything. I'm sure Samantha won't mind if I ask to borrow a few things to make her birthday cupcakes. I'm playing it smart: I'm going to bake my sister's cupcakes at her cabin, *not* beforehand. I don't want to drive up the bumpy mountain road with the cupcakes, like I did last year. They ended up being jumbled in their box and were a mess once I arrived.

I love baking cupcakes.

I *loathe* traveling with cupcakes.

It's one of the most stressful parts of being a baker. I work all day on an amazing wedding cupcake display, but then I have to box everything up and safely move it to the venue: complete nightmare. Luckily, I don't do that very often. Working at a tiny bakery in a remote mountain town means we don't get many fancy wedding cupcake orders. I went to culinary school and did an apprenticeship in the city, but now I'm finally home, and have been for the past year.

Gwen, the owner of Bliss Cupcakes & Café, was happy to hire me on, especially with all my 'big city training'. She often questions why I even came back to the tiny little mountain town of Blytheton, but this is *home*. It's where my older sisters are. It's where I have all the memories of my parents, tucked away, safe. It's where I belong.

I glance at the clock on my stove and realize it's already four o'clock and I should be leaving. But then my phone dings, signaling a message from the Mountain Mates dating app. My sister Mallory was the one who suggested it, since she knows I've been pining for a special someone of my own. I'm low-key jealous every time I see her with her amazing husband, who she met on the app. It just feels like I have *nearly* everything, and I feel ready. I'm twenty-two. I've finished school. I've come back to Blytheton, where I belong. I have my dream job, with a wonderful boss. But I want more. I want, you know, the icing on the cupcake: a partner. My other half. The love of my life. The opportunity to start a family of my own. And I want it here, in my hometown, where the rest of my friends and family are.

I've been talking to a man named Dan on the app. I'm pansexual, and my profile says so, but so far, I've only received messages from men. Every time I get a new message from a man, I feel a little bit disappointed...and wonder if I'm full stop sapphic and not pan at all. The man who is currently messaging me is a lawyer named Dan. He says he's ready to quit the big city hustle. He wants the quiet life and to settle down. We've talked about these things, our hopes and dreams, and how we both want to have children within the next ten years or so. He's conventionally handsome, with thick dark hair and a strong jawline. My stomach flutters with nervous excitement as I open his newest message:

Dan: *Hey baby, you know what would make my day? Seeing pictures of you. All of you.*

And now my stomach plummets. *Is he asking me to send him nudes?* We've been chatting for a month. We've covered a lot of important material, and I felt a growing attachment. If he asked if he could come out and visit me, I would have typed back yes in a flash. But send him nudes? I've never sent nudes to anyone before. I don't know if I like the idea of having nude photos of myself out there in the world. We haven't even sexted yet. And I haven't told him I'm a virgin. Before I can even type back, my phone dings again with another message from Dan.

Dan: *Help me take care of this, future wifey?*

And then there's a close-up picture of his erect penis. I gasp and nearly drop my phone in shock. My virginal eyes were not ready for that. I quickly hit delete and turn off the phone, just as I hear a quick *honk-honk* from below my apartment's window. I live above the bakery, on the main strip of town. Looking out my window, I see Lora's beat up gray pickup truck, parked and idling at the side of the road. Lora has been best friends with my oldest sister, Samantha, since they were toddlers.

I toss my backpack over my shoulder, pick up my box of baking supplies, and hurry out the door. As I reach the street, Lora is now waiting next to the passenger side door, leaning up against her truck, ankles crossed. She's wearing a blue plaid shirt with a pair of dark denim overalls that aren't quite baggy, but they aren't fitted either. They just *casually* hug her curves. Her dark brown hair is worn in a braid, draping over one shoulder, and her arms are crossed over her chest. She's usually all smiles and talkative with Samantha, but she's always a bit grumpy with me, even when she stops by the café for her daily lunchtime tea and cupcake. At the moment, she's probably annoyed that she has to drive Little Nelly up the mountain *again*, because I still don't have a truck of my own, Mallory is busy with opening week at the mountain summer camp she runs with her husband, and Samantha got called in to work an extra shift with the Mountain Rescue team. Lora runs the town's grocery store, now that her parents have retired, so she was available and nearby.

"You're late," Lora says, but flings the passenger side door open for me.

"I'm like one minute late," I argue. "You said you'd be here at four–"

"It's three past four," she says. Her voice is flat, and I have no idea if she's joking or deadly serious.

I huff and toss my bag in the backseat, followed by my box of supplies, before climbing in. She slams the door, causing me to jump. *Is she seriously this angry about me being three minutes late?* I feel on edge, sitting in Lora's truck and thinking about the long drive up the mountain with someone who is annoyed with me. It's not helping that I still feel queasy about the messages from Dan. I thought we had something–something real. I thought there was some sort of understanding that I wasn't the type of girl who was ready for nude requests, followed by cock shots. My phone dings again, just as Lora pulls away from the curb.

"Storm's coming," Lora says. "We'll be lucky if we beat it."

"And if we left three minutes ago, we would have?" I ask.

"Only time will tell. What is all that stuff you shoved in the back?"

"Baking supplies," I say.

"For what?"

"Baking."

We're driving along the main street, Lora's eyes focused on the road, but I catch her giving me a quick and annoyed-looking side glance.

"It's for Samantha's birthday cupcakes," I explain.

"Why didn't you bake them in the fancy bakery you work at?" she asks.

Bliss Cupcakes & Café is a far cry from fancy, but I don't correct her.

"I hate traveling with cupcakes," I say. "I tried it last year. Big disaster."

"Maybe that's because Mallory drove you up the mountain," Lora says.

"My sister is a perfectly competent driver," I say.

I glance at Lora, and see her brow crinkling in thought, her dark blue eyes still looking ahead at the road.

"I don't remember there being a cupcake disaster last year," she says.

"I fixed it. Or as best as I could," I say. "Sometimes you can work miracles with icing. But I'd rather not relive the experience."

"I don't think Samantha cares about how fancy her birthday cupcakes are."

"*I* care," I say. "I like making cupcakes for people I love. It's my favorite kind of cupcake to bake. It's not like I'm making a five-tier wedding cupcake display with over a hundred fondant roses, but I still want them to be good, tasty cupcakes."

Lora grunts, and I see a bit of pink color her cheeks. I look out my window at the passing trees, as we turn off the main road and begin our drive up the mountain. I really don't feel like trying to pull a conversation from Lora. I'd rather have both of us brood in silence the whole ride. Anyway, how exactly do you explain to your older sister's

BFF that you're currently suffering from cock shock and don't feel like talking?

I shift in my seat, curling my shoulder inward and cutting myself off from Lora, as I pull out my phone. I open the app to see if there are any new messages or pictures from Dan. Unfortunately, there is one message waiting.

Dan: *Baby, I'm waiting.*

I scowl and turn my phone off. He's going to be waiting a *long* time, because I am not sending nudes to him, or anyone else, ever.

Chapter Two: Lora

Tasty cupcakes. I bet Nelly tastes like tasty vanilla cream cupcakes...

I really need to stop thinking...thoughts. It's hard, when this cute blonde is sitting so close to me, making the whole truck smell like confetti cupcakes. I'm not sure if it's the supplies she packed, or if it's her. But I want to find out. I want to find out what she tastes like.

Yep, there's those pesky sex-thoughts again.

I go through my list, the one I've been adding to ever since she moved back home a few months ago, the one detailing all the reasons I can never actually find out what Nelly tastes like.

Number one: she's my best friend's little sister.

Number two: she's a sweet, angelic cupcake of a human being.

Number three: and my default setting is grumpy, recluse mountain woman.

Number four: she's my best friend's little sister.

Number five: she's a decade younger than me.

Number six: she's my best friend's little sister.

Number seven: I have no clue if she even likes women.

Number eight: she's my best friend's little sister.

And on top of that, most of Samantha's friends treat Nelly like a little sister, since most of the mountain folk helped Samantha raise her two younger sisters after their parents died. Samantha was eighteen, and the girls didn't have any other relations, so she took custody of eight-year-old Nelly and twelve-year-old Mallory. I try not to picture eight-year-old Nelly, because that's a little weird. I knew her as a little girl when I was a teenager, but as far as I'm concerned, that was over a dozen years ago, so basically, it's ancient history. I do not see her as a little sister. I see her as the beautiful blonde woman sitting next to me, who always smells like cupcakes.

But something's off today. Even though I'm a bit gruff and short with her, she usually playfully banters back, as if to tease me. It's kind of become our thing. There is no reason for me to leave the grocery store every day at noon, not with the perfectly good coffee machine and tea collection in our break room and the fully stocked grocery shelves, but I go down to Bliss Cupcakes & Café every Monday through Friday for my lunchtime tea fix and one of Nelly's delicious-as-fuck confetti cupcakes. I know, it's not a very mature flavor. It's the kind of cupcake most often used for children's birthday parties. But I crave them, just as much as I crave hearing her voice and seeing her smile and letting her tease me about my childish cupcake choice. But there's no teasing today. She's turned away from me, clutching her phone and looking out her window.

My attention is pulled away from her as a few drops of rain patter onto the windshield. Then more fall, forcing me to click the windshield wipers on.

"See?" I say. "Storm is here."

The sky has grown dark. We're driving up the twisting mountain road, trees thick on each side of us, blocking out what little sun was left in the day, and now the storm has rolled in, taking care of the final rays of sunshine.

"It's just a little rain," Nelly says.

Lightning flashes, followed by the crack of thunder. I look over at her, raising one eyebrow: *I was right.* It's going to be a full-blown storm.

She huffs, crossing her arms over her chest. I glance over, taking in her little cutoff denim shorts and the smooth expanse of lightly tanned skin, from thigh to ankle. She's the kind of beautiful that blends well with adorable, and which also happens to be my weakness when it comes to women. Time to go over that list again:

Number one: she's my best friend's little sister.

Number two: *is that a fucking tree?*

I slam on the brakes, desperate not to smash into the giant tree that has just crashed down across the road, directly in front of us. Nelly screams as I swerve on the rain drenched road, but I manage to safely stop the truck without smashing into anything. I look out at the massive tree now blocking our path, my heart pounding. I inhale deeply, steadying my breath, and inhale that sweet cupcake scent and remember Nelly is with me.

"You okay?" I ask, turning to Nelly.

She's gripping the seatbelt across her chest, white knuckled, brown eyes gone wide, and breathing heavily.

"Nelly?" I try again, unclipping myself so I can reach over.

I cup her face in my hands, trying to look into her eyes, but she looks dazed, not quite focusing on anything.

"Nelly? You okay?" I ask. "Talk to me."

She lets out a gasp and her eyes focus on me. "I'm okay. I was just...a little shocked. But I'm okay."

I pat her cheek, smiling in relief. "Good girl."

She blinks, her cheeks flushing pink, the color traveling all the way up to her ears. I'm still cradling her face in my hands as I glance down to her plump, pink lips, slightly parted as her breathing returns to normal. *I could kiss her.* I'm so relieved she's okay, I could kiss her. My heart is racing. Because of the tree. The sudden stop. The relief that she's okay. And because I want to kiss her so damn badly.

Chapter Three:
Nelly

I'm sitting in the truck, half in shock because we almost crashed, and half in shock because Lora's hands are touching me so gently it makes my heart feel utterly confused. And it looks like she's going to kiss me. Her face is so close to mine. She smells fresh and alive, like a pretty blend of spearmint and petrichor.

Rain taps steadily on the roof of the truck, and this would almost be romantic if it wasn't Grumpy Lora, staring into my soul with her dark blue eyes. But has she always had those thick, long lashes? And did Lora just call me a *good girl*? And why does that make me feel tight in all the good ways, a heat suddenly building in my core?

"Good girl..." Lora repeats absently with a nod, and then blinks, seeming to come to her senses. She quickly removes her hands and shifts away from me, like my skin is a hot pancake skillet.

"I'm gonna' go look at that tree," Lora says. "Stay here."

It's like she can't leap out of the truck fast enough, jumping head-first into the torrential downpour. She returns a moment later, soaked through, dark hair plastered to her skull.

"Well?" I ask. "Report?"

Lightning flashes, helpfully shedding light on the massive tree blocking our path, followed by deafening thunder.

"So...that's a really big tree," Lora says, stating the obvious. "And there are too many trees on either side of the road to get around."

"Should we call for help?" I ask.

Lora shakes her head. "You grew up here. You know cell service is shit during storms."

I nod. "I wouldn't want to ask anyone to come out here anyway, putting themselves in danger, too."

"What are you suggesting?" Lora asks, sounding as grumpy as ever.

"We hunker down here for the night?" I suggest. *What else are we supposed to do?* We don't have phone service. The rain is coming down in sheets. The road is completely blocked by a giant tree.

Lora looks back out at the tree, looking pensive. "You know, my cabin isn't that far. We could walk the rest of the way, then get warmed up by the fire. Beats sitting out here all night."

"Yeah?" I ask. "Are you sure it's not that far?"

I've never been to Lora's cabin. I've been to her parents' place, when I was younger and they used to occasionally watch me when Samantha was working, but I've never been to Lora's home.

Lora shakes her head. "Are you questioning how well I know this mountain?"

"Oh, heaven forbid," I say, rolling my eyes. But I look back at my baking supplies, wondering how they will fare during a rainstorm hike. "I packed my baking stuff in a cardboard box. It's going to get soaked."

"You expect us to haul your box of cupcake stuff to my cabin?" Lora asks.

"You said it's not far!" I argue. "And I need to bake Samantha's birthday cupcakes!"

I feel a slight panic setting into my bones. I should have already baked the damn cupcakes and just risked the drive up. I could have at least had all the little cakes baked, and then maybe decorated them once I got to Samantha's. *Why didn't I think of that yesterday?*

"You have to bake the cupcakes tonight?" Lora asks.

"That was the plan," I say. "Just...at Samantha's cabin, not yours."

Lora lets out a long sigh. "I have a tarp and a flashlight in the back. Let me get them."

Lora returns shortly with a bright blue waterproof tarp and hands me the flashlight. She's silent as she studiously wraps the tarp around my box of baking supplies. She hefts the box into her arms, which I assume means she's offering to carry it. I swing my backpack onto my shoulders and follow her as she sets off into the dark and rain drenched forest, and I sincerely hope she knows what she's doing.

"Not far my ass," I grumble.

We've been walking for ten minutes. In my mind, anything longer than ten minutes should be labeled as *far*, especially if you're hiking uphill in the dark while ice cold rain pours down your shirt. I'm wearing denim cutoffs, so my bare legs are freezing, and my socks squelch in my sneakers with every icy-cold step.

"Not much longer, I swear," Lora says. "Just round this bend is my driveway."

Right, her driveway; her driveway that snakes through the trees for another half mile. I feel bone-aching relief as we round the final bend, and a quaint cabin comes into view. We rush inside, sopping wet and dripping on the hardwood floors.

"I'll get the fire started," she says, dumping the tarp-covered box on her rustic kitchen table and going to tend the fireplace.

Her cabin is essentially one big, open space. There's electricity, a fully functional kitchen, with a bathroom tucked off the side. There's a couch in front of the central fireplace, and a tall dresser and large bed tucked into the corner. Across the mantle of the fireplace are stacks of paperback books. They all look old, the edges of their pages yellowed, and most of them are sporting cracked spines.

I look through my backpack, only to find everything I packed is drenched. But there was only one tarp. It was more important to protect the cupcake ingredients. The clothes I packed will dry eventually.

When I look up, Lora has the fire going and is chucking off her overalls, stripping down to her underwear and her long plaid shirt. She catches my eye as she unfolds a laundry rack near the fire, hanging her overalls on it.

"I'll get us towels," Lora says, and disappears into the bathroom.

She quickly returns, wrapped in a cozy-looking blue housecoat, and hands me a fluffy towel.

"You should take your clothes off," Lora says.

"W-what?" I ask, suddenly freezing, lips chattering.

She nods to the bathroom. "You need to get changed."

"I have nothing dry to put on."

She sighs and goes to her dresser, pulling out a red flannel nightshirt and a pair of thick gray socks.

"This okay?" Lora asks, holding them out to me. "I'm thinking all my pants will be a bit big on you..."

"It's fine," I tell her hurriedly. "Perfect."

I turn away, heading into the bathroom. With trembling, freezing hands, I peel my rain drenched clothes off, and then dry myself off with the towel. I pull the nightshirt on and button it up, inhaling deeply. And there's that minty petrichor scent again. I really wish I didn't love that smell so much. Because it's Lora. My eldest sister's best friend. A woman who will only ever see me as Little Nelly. It feels like I'm constantly wearing a big neon sign that says, "Do not touch!" at all times. And Lora's never dated anyone, at least not that I know of. I have no idea what her preferences are.

My mind wanders back to Dan, and I wonder if he's sent me more dick pics, or if he's given up. I want to check the app. But mostly because I've decided I want to tell him to go fuck himself and take care of his hard on without my help. But I'm not sure if Lora has an internet connection in her cabin, or if it would even work during the storm.

The shirt falls to my knees, and I vaguely wonder if I should have asked Lora for a pair of underwear. She's definitely curvier than me, but wearing nothing feels...unnatural. I always wear underwear, even when I go to bed. However, going without feels...a little bit sexy. We're alone. In this cabin. With one bed. But I try to push those thoughts away as I put on the socks, pulling them all the way up to my knees.

I'm still trying to push sexy thoughts away as I step out of the bathroom and I'm greeted by a lovely view of Lora's ass, being artfully illuminated by the light of the fire. She turns in surprise and–

"I'm sorry!" I shout, covering my eyes. She's completely naked. Apparently, she decided to change out of the housecoat. And apparently, she expected me to take longer in the bathroom.

I continue to stand frozen to the spot, my hands covering my eyes, breathing heavily. I have no idea what to do. I'm waiting for some guidance, anything. Should I just retreat into the bathroom? Is she going to say anything? Is she going to tell me when she's done getting dressed so I can unfreeze and forget this ever happened? Am I completely overreacting? We're both women. This is just like getting changed in a locker room, right? Then why doesn't it feel that way?

Chapter Four: Lora

With her arms raised, covering her eyes, the hem of my shirt she's wearing is just about to uncover *her*. I didn't give her underwear. I thought it'd be weird to give her a pair of underwear, and like I said about bottoms, they'd probably be too big. She's slimmer than me, with narrow hips, a barely there ass, and tiny breasts. But now I'm re-thinking my decision to not lend her underwear. I should have given her *something*. Anything. I *shouldn't* have given this beautiful young woman a little nightshirt and a pair of socks and *nothing* else. I am all too aware that if she lifted her hands a bit higher, or if that shirt was just a bit shorter, I'd be getting the same full-frontal view she just got of me. She's got the socks pulled up to her knees, but somehow that's sexy. There's just the smooth, pale skin of her hips and thighs on display and I like what I see. I want to sink my fingertips into her hips, feel those thighs wrapped around me and–

Oh yeah, I'm still naked. And I feel heat throbbing in my pussy.

"Give me a minute!" I shout, frantically shoving my legs into my underwear and pulling on my gray sweatpants, a comfy bralette, and a sweatshirt.

"I'm so sorry!" Nelly says, still completely frozen with her hands over her eyes.

The way she's freaking out, it's like she's never seen anyone naked before. *Has she never seen anyone naked before?* I know she gives off the sweet, innocent vibes, the very thing that makes my pussy ache, but that can't be completely true. She went to school and lived in the city for five years. She must have had boyfriends, or at least one. Or girlfriends. God, I wish I knew what she was into. All I know is there is no fucking way this gorgeous young woman is a virgin. But...I do kind of like the thought of that. She'd be mine and only mine. Maybe no one else has ever touched her, made her feel good. I could do that. I could make her feel good. *The list.* I need to go through my list. I take a few deep breaths, reciting the list in my head, and then tell her to go ahead and open her eyes.

"I am so sorry," Nelly says again, taking a few tentative steps forward.

"C'mon, get warmed up by the fire," I tell her. I don't want to keep dwelling on it.

She obeys, taking a seat on the couch in front of the fire and curling her feet under her. I want to go sit next to her. I want to pull her into me, cradling her back against my chest, and make sure she's thoroughly warmed up.

"You want something to eat?" I ask instead, heading into the kitchen. "I can make us some sandwiches."

"Sure," she says. "And I still need to make Samantha's cupcakes, if that's okay?"

"You're sure?" I ask. "We still have to drive them up the mountain tomorrow. That is, if someone manages to move the tree by then."

I open the fridge and get out some cheese slices and lunch meat, along with some mayo. If I knew I was going to be entertaining someone, I would have been more prepared in the food department, but this will have to do. I can't believe I manage a grocery store and I only have cold cuts to offer.

"I don't want to leave Samantha's cupcakes until the last minute," Nelly says. "And the plan was to let them cool overnight, and then ice them in the morning."

"You're the baking queen," I say, slathering mayo on some bread and putting together the depressing dinner of a bachelorette. I slap on the meat and cheese and then place the sandwiches on plates.

"Coffee? Tea?" I ask. "Something to help you warm up?"

"Do you actually have tea?" Nelly asks.

"I actually have tea," I say, a slow smile playing at my lips. I go to my tea cupboard, looking over the wide selection of teas I've curated over the years: bags and tins and little wooden boxes, all full of loose-leaf tea and neatly packaged tea bags. I'm kind of a crazy tea lady. I may not be able to offer a nice dinner, but maybe Nelly will be impressed by my tea collection.

"Well, what kind of tea do you have?" Nelly asks.

"Do you want caffeine or no caffeine?" I ask.

She narrows her eyes, taking in the cupboard. "Is that an *entire cupboard* full of tea?"

"It is."

Slowly, she stands up, as if in awe, and walks over. She's so close I can smell that sweet cupcake smell on her again. Even after being drenched in the rain and dressed in my clothes, her own smell still clings to her.

"What is...Guangzhou milk oolong?" Nelly asks, pointing to one of the boxes.

"It's, um...a smooth and creamy Chinese tea," I explain. "Medium caffeine."

I'm not making it up. It actually says *smooth and creamy* on the packaging. But she turns to look at me, a small smile on her luscious lips, before returning her attention back to the tea cupboard.

"And Japanese Sencha? What's that?"

"A traditional green tea," I tell her. "It has that strong, fresh grass taste to it, so if you don't like green tea–"

"I like green tea," Nelly says. "Can I try that one?"

"Of course," I say. "I'll put the kettle on."

An hour later, we've eaten our dinner, sitting on opposite sides of the couch, and are finishing off the last dregs of our tea. She holds her phone, checking it, but is obviously unhappy with what she finds.

"Sorry, I don't have Wi-Fi up here," I tell her. I mean, I live in a cabin in the woods for a reason. I like the rustic life. I have electricity, indoor plumbing, and a kitchen, but I prefer to be tech free. Besides, I have to go to work at the grocery store nearly every day, and we have Wi-Fi down there.

"Yeah, and my data isn't working," she says. "Phone signal is also out."

"Were you expecting a message?" I ask. "Or just trying to call Samantha to let her know where you are?"

"A bit of both," she says. "Hopefully Samantha will figure out we decided not to travel tonight in the storm and haven't been able to call."

"Hopefully," I say.

"And I was on that stupid dating app..." Nelly mumbles.

"What stupid dating app?" I ask.

"The one Mallory is always going on about because it's how she met her husband," Nelly says. "Mountain Mates? Have you heard of it?"

I shake my head. And try not to be too upset by the fact that she's on a dating app. Talking to people. Other people. People who aren't me.

"What is this dating app?" I ask.

"It's like...matching city folk with small town mountain folk, like us," Nelly explains. "City folk who are overwhelmed by city life and just want to run away to the mountains, but want it to be this big romantic thing with a new love and a new life. But I think it works better for guys."

"Why do you say that?" I ask, genuinely curious.

"I don't want to sound sexist, but I think city girls like the idea of being swept off their feet by a burly mountain man, tucked away in his cabin away from the city, ready to make babies and live happily ever after together," Nelly says wistfully. "While city guys...what exactly is the fantasy there? They meet a fair maiden who lives in the mountains and they...what? Move into her quaint cottage and have to learn how to chop wood and stuff? It somehow feels a little less appealing from that perspective. So, it's no wonder I barely get any matches from guys or girls, and anytime I actually do, they ghost me after just a few messages."

I swear my heart skips a beat when she says guys *or girls*, but I try to play it cool.

"Their loss," I tell her. "Why are you even on an app? Why not just meet someone in person?"

She shakes her head, frowning.

"Because around these parts, I'll always be Little Nelly," she says. "The people on this mountain helped raise me, including you. You see me as Samantha and Mallory's little sister and nothing else. I feel like living here is like wearing a chastity belt, and no one is willing to take a chance unlocking it, for fear of Samantha's wrath. And yet...I can't imagine living anywhere else, so I had to come back."

She has a point. It's actually multiple points on my list, which I need to go over again, because she looks so sad and defeated and because she said she's interested in girls. I want to wrap her in a hug and tell her everything is going to be okay. Because she could be mine. If she was just a regular girl, *not* Samantha's little sister, she'd already be mine. I feel sure of it.

"What about when you lived in the city?" I ask, because I desperately want to know. "You must have dated someone then? No one would see you as Samantha's little sister there."

Nelly shrugs. "No one ever seemed interested."

I laugh, shaking my head. "How could they not–"

But I stop myself because her cheeks are growing pink again. And she's biting her bottom lip, her eyes making quick glances from me to the fire, and then back again.

"How could they not what...?" she asks, quietly.

"Not see how beautiful you are," I say, just as hushed.

"You have to say that," Nelly says. "You're one of the people who looks at me and sees a kid sister."

"That is definitely not what I see," I say.

Am I even reading this right? Is she looking for compliments because she's feeling sad and unwanted by whatever loser just ghosted her on that stupid app, or is she fishing to see if I'm into her? Is there any possibility that she is even remotely into me?

She shifts on the couch, inching a little bit closer. I do the same until our knees are *just* touching. She looks down, her bare knee touching mine. I can feel her warmth, even through my sweatpants.

I decide to take a chance. I reach out, grazing my knuckle on her knee. And her whole body gets tense.

"Samantha's cupcakes!" Nelly says, jumping to her feet. "Oh my god, I have to make her birthday cupcakes!"

She rushes into the kitchen, and I let out a long sigh. So much for that.

CHAPTER FIVE: NELLY

Yes, baking birthday cupcakes for my sister is the *perfect* distraction for whatever was about to happen on Lora's couch. She touched me. It made me melt. It was just her knuckle on my knee, and it made me feel like my insides were burning, melting, sparking...all of the above and everything else.

I unpack my supplies from my box and notice my hands are trembling slightly. I take a deep breath, steadying them, before I unpack the rest. Most of the stuff is pretty dry, thankfully. Lora pushes herself off the couch, walking over and leaning on the kitchen counter just a few feet away.

"Can I help?" she asks.

"Have you ever baked cupcakes?"

Lora laughs. "No. Teach me?"

Good god, why is this beautiful woman sincerely asking me to teach her how to bake the cause of so much inner melting? I swallow, unable to look over at her. I can feel her eyes on me, watching my every move. I remove the main mixing bowl and my handheld mixer, desperately trying to assess my current situation.

"May I?" I ask, pointing to the oven. "It needs to be preheated."

"It's all yours," Lora says.

I turn the oven on and then return to the counter.

"Well, first we mix the dry ingredients," I tell Lora. "We're going to use two cups of flour…"

I go through the process of mixing the dry, Lora watching intently the entire time.

"Then we're going to mix the wet," I say, grabbing another bowl.

"Mmmhmm," she says.

I bite my lip, pausing as I try to recall what ingredients I need next. I can bake cupcakes from heart. I don't usually need a recipe, but suddenly my mind has gone blank. And baking cupcakes has never been a sexually taut experience. And it's cupcakes for my *sister*. So why do I feel so amped up? Just because Lora's watching my every move, her gaze hooded and focused?

Then I remember what I need: "Do you have any eggs? I probably should have asked that sooner…Oh, and milk. And butter. Sorry."

If I wasn't so flustered I would have made sure she had everything before I started.

"I have eggs," Lora says. "And milk and butter."

Lora pushes herself off the counter. She has to walk behind me to get to the fridge. I feel the light touch of her fingers brushing my back as she passes. The touch is over before it's even begun, but I feel myself wanting more. I want her hands on the small of my back. On my waist. My hips.

"How many eggs?" she asks, standing with the fridge open.

"Two, please."

Lora takes out two eggs and hands them over to me, letting our fingers briefly touch. She places a carton of milk and a small pat of butter on the counter. I glance up at her and see she's smiling warmly.

"I like watching you in your element," she says. "What's next?"

"Sugar," I say. I crack the eggs and toss the shells, and then reach for my tin of sugar. I feel her eyes on me the entire time.

"And then?"

"Vanilla," I say, picking up the bottle and carefully measuring it into my measuring spoon.

I carry on, hyperaware of her eyes on me the entire time. I pour the wet into the dry and grab my mixer, mixing all the ingredients into a nice, cream colored cupcake batter. It's just basic vanilla cupcakes, but it's always been Samantha's favorite, so it's what I make for her every year. Satisfied that I'm done, I click the mixer off. Before I can even reach for the cupcake pans, Lora is handing them to me.

"Thank you," I say.

"Do we get to lick the beaters now?" she asks.

"There's raw egg in this!" I tell her. "And most people don't realize it, but you can also get salmonella poisoning from raw flour."

"Yeah, but my mom *always* let me lick the beaters when she was baking a cake," she tells me with a grin. "And I never got sick."

And well, yes, my mom always let me and my sisters lick the beaters. And we never got sick. But I'm an adult now. I don't lick cake beaters. I give Lora a small smile and shake my head, and then turn away to focus on portioning the batter into the cupcake pans. Lora hands me my spatula from my box of supplies, just as I need it. I thank her and get every last bit of batter into the pans, just as the oven beeps to let us know it's sufficiently heated. I turn away to put the pans in the oven when I hear a distinct click. I spin around only to find Lora releasing the beaters, holding one in each hand. She holds one towards me, smiling playfully.

"Lora, do not lick that beater!" I tell her.

Lick.

She runs her tongue up one of the prongs, still offering me the other. I roll my eyes and accept. I take a tentative lick, holding her gaze. And okay, maybe I've been missing out. Maybe I should lick the beaters clean more often. It's not something I'd do at work, but maybe I can do it at home. Fingers crossed we don't get salmonella poisoning and spend the rest of the night sick.

A friend at culinary school once told me: *never make eye contact while eating a banana.* I guess the same is true for licking baking utensils. I feel my cheeks grow hot as Lora expertly cleans hers, using her tongue to get around all the spokes. I hesitantly lick the sweet batter, acutely aware that she's watching every single lick of my tongue, and I feel a lightness in my chest, my heart beating wildly.

Chapter Six: Lora

God, Nelly is fucking hot. I can't take my eyes off her as she licks her utensil clean. I finish mine, tossing it in the mixing bowl, and then step forward and pluck hers away, tossing it in the bowl even though she isn't quite done.

She opens her mouth to protest but shuts it again as I close the distance between us, her big brown eyes zeroing in on my lips. I give her a minute for her brain to acknowledge what I'm about to do, and when she doesn't make a move to back away, I kiss her. She tastes like cupcakes. She makes a surprised noise, something between a gasp and a moan. Then she's kissing me back, her tongue tentatively meeting mine, her soft body melting against me. I grip her by the waist and hoist her up onto the counter, and she parts her legs, making room for me, her hands resting on my shoulders.

One whole year. The entire year she's been back in town, I've been dying to know what she tastes like.

"Lora...?" she asks, sounding just as bewildered as I feel.

"I *do not* see you as Little Nelly," I tell her, my hands still firmly on her waist. "Is that okay with you?"

She visibly swallows, but her pretty pink lips part and she nods. She threads her fingers into my still-damp hair, pulling me in for another kiss. I moan, wanting to devour every sweet inch of her, wanting to taste all of her. I hoist her up, our lips still locked, and she wraps her legs and arms around me.

"You're stronger than you look!" Nelly gasps.

"And you're pretty damn small," I tell her, nuzzling into the soft skin of her neck.

I relocate us to the couch and plop down, Nelly straddling me. She pulls back, tracing a finger down my face.

"Grumpy Lora..." she says, a smile pulling at her sweet lips.

"Yes, Nelly?" I ask, not entirely thrilled with that nickname.

"I just...all this time, I thought you despised me," she says.

"I could never despise you," I tell her, taking her hand from my face so I can kiss her palm. "I was just so goddamn mad that you were off limits."

She bites her lip. "Am I still off limits?"

"I caved," I tell her. "I couldn't stand being around you any longer and not knowing what it was like to kiss you."

"And Samantha...?"

"As far as I'm concerned, your big sister is a million miles away."

"She's just up the mountain," Nelly says.

"But do you like this?" I ask, and go in for another kiss, her lips tasting just as sweet as the first time.

She moans into our kiss. She feels so soft and warm.

"I'm going to take that as a yes," I tell her. Then, softly: "Can I touch you?"

"Y-yes..." Nelly says.

We've parted our kiss so I can look at her. I hold her gaze as I reach down, and remember she's not wearing any underwear. Her folds are slick and warm. A breath hitches in her throat as my fingers graze her clit and a pink blush colours her cheeks.

"Have you ever...?" I ask, gently caressing her clit. She shivers, squirming under my touch, and shakes her head.

"But you want this?" I ask.

She nods enthusiastically.

"But I've never done this," she says. "Teach me?"

I grin and reach up to tuck a long lock of blonde hair behind her ear, so I can see her pretty face and her big brown eyes.

"This isn't like baking cupcakes," I tell her. "There's no recipe, no instructions. We just do what feels good."

For emphasis, I slowly push a single finger into her, and she shudders, eyes closing, her teeth clenched.

"Does that feel good?" I ask her.

"Yes," Nelly answers. "But..."

"But what, sweetness?"

"I just..." I wait patiently as she fumbles for her words. All the while she slowly, tentatively undulates her hips against my touch, eyes shut, her pussy warm and slick.

"Just what?" I ask.

Nelly opens her eyes and blinks. "I just don't know if...I'm going to do it right? And make you feel good, too?"

"We can take our time," I tell her. "You tell me what feels good, and I'll let you know the same."

We can take all the time in the world we need, because I'm certain I don't want anyone else. Ever.

CHAPTER SEVEN: NELLY

"I don't want to take it slow," I tell Lora. I wrap my arms around her, my lips meeting her neck, kissing, exploring.

It feels like my body is coming alive and unraveling all at the same time, and all I can clearly focus on is her gentle touch, coaxing me to completely come undone. This is Lora. I've known her pretty face, kind blue eyes, and long brown hair my whole life. And I've never really believed in soulmates or fate, but feeling her body pressed against mine suddenly makes all the sense in the world. This is it. This is fucking everything. I am *home*, exactly where I'm meant to be, and I want her. All of her. I want her to have all of me.

I reach down for the hem of my nightshirt and pull it over my head, tossing it to the floor. Lora inhales sharply, her eyes eagerly drinking in the sight of my small but perky breasts. She slowly drags her finger out of my soaking wet pussy so she can palm my breasts, circling my wetness around one taut nipple with the tip of her finger. She holds my gaze as she slips her finger inside of me again, gathering up more of my wetness, and then applies it to my other nipple, massaging my breasts and making my nipples glisten in the firelight. I arch my back, relishing her touch. And then she leans in, her soft, warm lips suckling me, her tongue wiping my juices clean from my sensitive flesh. My pussy throbs more with every lap of her tongue.

"Fuck, you taste good..." Lora moans.

I tug at her shirt. "Can I see you?"

"Yes," she says, but she's kissing my breasts again, making me whimper and throb and pant. I playfully growl at her, tugging at her sweatshirt, until she relents and lets her lips part from my skin so I can pull it off. I immediately return the favor, exploring her nipples with my tongue, breathing in her fresh, clean scent. I glance up and see her head has rolled back, eyes closed, a small smile on her lips. And remind myself I shouldn't be so nervous, because this is Lora. This isn't some douchebag city lawyer on an app sending me dick pics. This isn't one of the countless people who I chatted with, only to be ghosted. Lora's the real thing. She's so real I can feel the warmth of her body beneath me. I pause tasting her skin so I can rest my head against her chest, just above her ample breasts, and listen to the steady thump of her heart.

I feel her sigh, and then Lora's running her fingers through my hair, then slowly down each ridge of my spine, until she reaches my ass, and her touch goes from gentle to urgent, squeezing and pulling me in closer for a hungry kiss.

"See?" Lora says, playfully biting my lower lip. "You don't need a teacher. You're a natural."

"But can we go to your bed?" I ask, feeling bold.

"Yes, sweetness," Lora says, grabbing my ass and standing, so I have to wrap my legs and arms around her again. "We can go to my bed."

Lora lays me down on my back. I part my legs for her, still wearing the knee-high socks. Lora's eyes drink in my thrumming pussy. She licks her lips.

"I want to taste more of you," Lora says.

I nod and she crawls forward, lowering her mouth to lick up my slit before sucking on my clit.

"Oh, fuck!" I gasp, my hands clenching the sheets, and then reaching for her. I can only reach the top of her head, and my fingers curl into her hair.

I've touched myself before. I know what it feels like to come, and I'm prepared to chase that feeling, but *fuck,* her mouth feels good. I squirm as Lora slips a finger into my entrance, her mouth still firmly focused on pleasuring my clit. With her free hand she grasps my inner thigh, holding me still while simultaneously pushing my leg wider. My fingers in her hair curl tighter and she moans into my pussy.

"F-fuck..." is all I manage to say before I start to feel myself coming completely undone.

Lora tentatively fucks another finger into me, pausing as I stretch around her. When my only response is another moan of pleasure, she resumes, fucking me harder with her fingers and kissing and sucking my clit, my entire body now slick with sweat. Lora only pauses again for a moment, just brief enough to look up at me. My eyes lock with hers, as she says, "Good girl, Nelly. You're getting fucked like such a good girl."

Her praise ignites me, and she continues to fuck me hard. I feel my orgasm slam into me, flowing from my pussy as I clench repeatedly around Lora's fingers, and into the rest of my body, down my limbs, and into my soul. Lora climbs up so she can kiss me, before collapsing onto me, but careful not to crush me. Our breaths come quick and short.

"That was…That was…" But before I can figure out words to describe what the hell just happened, the oven's timer beeps, signaling the cupcakes are ready.

Chapter Eight: Lora

"My cupcakes!" Nelly gasps. She pushes me off of her and I oblige, rolling onto my side.

Nelly scrambles out of bed, but then she gasps, crumpling to the ground.

"Nelly!" I cry. I rush over and crouch next to her, placing a hand on her shoulder. "Are you okay?"

I feel her shoulder shake beneath my touch, and for a sickening moment I think she's crying, until a laugh escapes her. She looks over at me, grinning and laughing.

"What?" I ask.

"My legs don't work," Nelly says, still laughing. "What did you do to me? I don't have any bones!"

I laugh with her, brushing her hair out of her face. "I'm pretty sure I fucked you until you saw stars."

"Yeah..." Nelly says, grinning. "You did do that."

I help Nelly to her feet, and she sits on the edge of the bed, still looking slightly sex-dazed, her blond hair an absolute mess.

"The cupcakes, Lora," she says, sounding sleepy. "Can you get the cupcakes out of the oven?"

"Of course," I say, giving her a kiss on her sweaty forehead before going to the kitchen.

I grab the potholders and remove the two pans of cupcakes, setting them down on top of the stove, knowing her eyes are watching me the whole time.

"Stick a knife in one, please," Nelly says. "If it comes out clean, it's good and done."

I do as she says and when I pull the knife out, it's clean as a whistle. I turn to her, giving her a thumbs up, but she's already fallen asleep, curled up on her side. I smile to myself, feeling pleased that I fucked her so thoroughly she's unable to stay conscious any longer. I don't mind that she didn't get a chance to return the favor, but I can't help but hope there'll be time for that sometime soon.

I turn off the oven and leave the cupcakes, making my way over to the bed. I pull my quilt over Nelly and then crawl into bed behind her, pulling her in close along my body.

When I wake just after dawn, Nelly's still peacefully sleeping. And while I'm eager to play with her again, I also want to know the status of the tree and if we're going to make it up to Samantha's in time for her birthday. I know Nelly has been looking forward to seeing her sisters, and I don't want her to be disappointed. I also don't want to wake her, when she's sleeping like this, all peaceful and adorable. So, I quietly slip out of bed and get dressed, making the hike back to the truck on my own. With any luck, I'll be tucked back into bed next to her when she wakes up, ready for round two.

It's still spitting out as I walk to where we left the truck. Being outside suddenly brings the world and reality back to me. We're no longer in my cozy cabin, just the two of us. Being outside, in the real world, makes me realize that, if Mountain Rescue did their job and cleared the tree, in just a few hours I'm going to be facing Samantha. The fact that I hear the buzz of chainsaws in the distance makes me think that's a genuine possibility.

I've been in love with my best friend's little sister for over a year. I finally let Nelly know and found out the feelings are mutual. I'd still be soaring along on Cloud Nine if I wasn't dreading coming face to face with Samantha and having to explain.

I reach the end of my drive and head down the main mountain road, the sound of chainsaws and woodchippers growing louder. As I round the bend, I see two members of Mountain Rescue at work: Levi and Jake.

"Lora," Levi says with a nod. "That's your truck, right?"

"Yep," I say. "You boys shorthanded? Need some help?"

"Samantha is off because it's her birthday weekend," Jake explains. "We don't mind. We figured we could tackle this ourselves, but if you want to lend a hand, we ain't stopping you."

"Seeing as you haven't cleared enough to get my truck down the road, looks like I'm pitching in," I say, rolling up my sleeves.

CHAPTER NINE: NELLY

When I wake up, Lora is gone. I reach a hand over to her side of the bed, feeling the cool sheets.

"Lora?" I call, looking over to the bathroom door, but it's wide open, and she isn't in there. It doesn't take long to take a quick survey of the rest of the cabin and realize she's not here.

My heart plummets and I feel a wave of dread flow through me. I wanted her to be here. I *expected* her to be here. And not just because I fell asleep wondering if she'd be okay with me returning the favor and going down on her before we left for the birthday party, but because...because that was my first time. I didn't expect Lora to be *gone*. I wanted to feel her warmth. Her arms around me. I wanted to be reassured that what we did last night meant something, but right now, waking up alone and feeling discarded, it kind of feels like a one-night-stand. It feels like I gave away my virginity to someone who just wanted to fool around, someone like Dick Pic Dan from the app. I thought Lora was different.

I get out of bed, thankful that my bones have now returned to my body, and the afterglow of sex has completely worn off. My pussy feels tender and sticky, but I'm able to walk to the bathroom and clean myself up. I retrieve my own clothes from the drying rack next to the dying fire and get dressed. I notice the phone service works again, so I make a quick phone call to Samantha, letting her know about the tree and that I'll hopefully see her later today.

Then I go check on the cupcakes. With a sigh, I remove them from the pan. They come out without a problem, and I get to work whipping up some icing. Hopefully, Lora has just gone to check on the truck situation. I suppose that would be a good reason to let me wake up alone, but I really wish she hadn't. I push that thought away and stir the vanilla icing. I want to have the cupcakes done before she gets back, so we can leave and make it to Samantha's place as soon as possible. I try to focus on the cupcakes, but the cabin smells more like sex than cupcakes at the moment, and I'm trying not to think about what happened last night and what exactly it meant to Lora.

I'm completely done icing the cupcakes and have even washed everything, packing it all back into my box, when Lora returns. She looks a bit disheveled, her plaid flannel shirt and jeans sprinkled with sawdust, and she grins when she sees me. I don't smile back.

"Morning," Lora says, walking over to the kitchen.

She reaches out to me, her hands brushing my waist, but I pick up my box of supplies and move away, carrying it to the door.

"Nelly?" she says, following me. "Something wrong?"

I turn to face her. "You left."

"You were sleeping," Lora says. "I wanted to be up early to help Mountain Rescue with removing that tree, so we can get to Samantha's. I didn't want to wake you."

I know it makes perfect sense, but I'm still feeling hurt. She *knew* it was my first time. I wanted to wake up in her arms, surrounded by her warmth, not completely alone in an empty cabin. I hug myself, looking down.

"Nelly?" she says, her knuckle tipping my chin up so I'm looking into her eyes. "Did I mess this up already?"

"I just expected you to be here," I tell her. "It was my first time and..." I swallow the lump in my throat, turning away. I have to blink to stop myself from crying. I feel like an idiot. A vulnerable, stupid idiot.

"I'm sorry," Lora says, her voice thick with emotion. "May I hug you?"

"No," I say. I know if she hugged me, I'd be engulfed in her fresh spearmint and petrichor scent. I know I'd end up wanting more. I already made that mistake once, and we do really need to get going to Samantha's. "Can we just leave?"

Chapter Ten: Lora

Nelly's quiet again. It feels like a repeat of our drive yesterday, but this time she isn't upset with some jerk on an app. She's upset with *me*. The rain is over, and the sun is shining, but I feel like I've tucked all the storm clouds inside my chest where my heart used to be. I know I fucked up by not being there when she woke up. I wasn't thinking straight. I feel like an idiot. And I already apologized, but I guess it wasn't enough. I'm hoping this means she just needs time, which I can give her. For now. Her confetti cupcake scent is filling the truck again and all I can think about is how delicious she tasted on my tongue and the soft, satisfied noises she made last night. I finally let her know how I feel. And then I immediately fucked it up. If I was nervous about having Samantha find out before I realized Nelly was upset with me, now I'm downright terrified of coming face to face with her big sister.

It's around lunchtime when we pull up to Samantha's cabin. It's much bigger than mine, since it was originally the family cabin built for two adults and their three daughters. Nelly technically still has her own room up here, but I know she prefers to live in her little apartment above the bakery, so she doesn't have to make the trip up and down the mountain every day. My mind drifts to how things would change if we really ended up together. I would build a new extension onto my cabin. Big enough for a family. But I can't get ahead of myself. She gave herself to me last night, but I don't know if she's thinking as long-term as I am, especially when she's still being sullen over this morning.

I smell barbecue as we get out of the truck. I head for the backyard, where I hear boisterous voices, but Nelly heads into the cabin, carrying Samantha's cupcakes in a white bakery box. I let her go. If I follow her, if I dote on her, Samantha is going to know in a second that I fucked things up. So instead, I round the corner to the backyard, where Samantha greets me with a big hug. I wave at Mallory and her husband Steve, who are currently tending the barbecue together.

"Lora!" Samantha says jovially. "Levi says you helped clear the road with Mountain Rescue this morning! You didn't have to do that. They could have called me."

"It's your birthday weekend," I argue. "I was happy to help."

Mallory walks over and offers me a cold beer, which I accept with a thanks.

"Where's Nelly?" Mallory asks. "I thought you were driving her up?"

I nod to the cabin. "Bringing the birthday cupcakes inside. I'm sure she'll be out in a minute."

But she isn't. Ten, twenty minutes pass. Then thirty, and I begin to worry. I catch Mallory's eye as she looks at the cabin, her brow furrowed.

"What's taking her so long?" Mallory asks.

I shrug and look away, taking a long pull from my beer. I'm at war with myself: should I keep giving Nelly space, or is she getting the wrong idea? Does she think I'm not interested? Should I go in and find her? But before I decide what to do, Mallory volunteers to go find her sister.

Chapter Eleven: Nelly

After dropping off the cupcakes in the kitchen, I really don't feel like going outside and facing the world; facing both my sisters and having Lora right there, pretending like nothing happened between us. Even if she meant every word she said, I don't know if I'm ready to let everyone else know about what happened between us.

I grab a granola bar and retreat to my old room. It looks the same as when I left it five years ago: same sky blue walls, same handmade quilt. I flop onto the bed, looking up at the white ceiling fan. I do an inventory of my body, wiggling my toes and fingers, feeling the slight soreness in my pussy. Do I feel different now that I've finally lost my virginity? *Should I feel different?*

My phone dings, interrupting my thoughts, and I find a message from Dan on the app.

Dan: *Still waiting, babe.*

Would sending a couple of nude pics be such a big deal? I kind of feel different about it now that I'm no longer a virgin. And I'm still kind of feeling upset about Lora ditching me and not being there when I woke up. And it's just a couple pics. I lift my shirt, exposing my breasts, and snap a picture. I turn my phone around, looking at the result and grimacing. They're not the most spectacular breasts. Lora seemed to appreciate them, but I'm not sure if Dan will be impressed. But before I can hit send, there's a knock at my door. I quickly pull my shirt back down and sit up.

"Who is it?" I call.

"Mallory."

"You can come in."

She opens the door slowly, looking around the room as if she'll figure out what's going on by my surroundings.

"You okay?" she asks.

"Yeah, fine," I lie. She sees right through it, obviously.

"Is this about that guy you've been messaging on the app?" she asks. "Did he ghost you?"

"No, not exactly," I say. "He just...asked for nudes. And sent me a dick pic."

Mallory wrinkles her nose. "Was there any sexy banter leading up to this or just...?"

"It kind of went from: what are your hobbies, what do you like about living in a small town, to here's my dick, send me nudes so I can jerk off. Is that normal? Is this how you do things on these apps?"

Mallory sits on the bed next to me. "I think normal behavior and acceptable behaviors are two wildly different things in this situation."

I nod, still clutching my phone. Mallory glances at it.

"So...did you?" she asks. "Did you send him nudes?"

"No," I say, shaking my head. "I don't think I want to. My boobs are just kind of...not that spectacular."

I make a purposeful look at her well-endowed chest and she shakes her head, laughing.

"Well, fuck that guy," Mallory says. "There are way more important things about you than your boobs. Besides, I happen to think they *are* spectacular."

I snort. "They're not."

"You know, big boobs are overrated," Mallory says. "If I'm not wearing a proper, squish-them-in-nice-and-tight sports bra, I have to actually hold them in place anytime I run. Just like, running to my car in a parking lot because it's raining: gotta' hold my boobs. Do you have any idea how ridiculous that looks?"

I laugh, shaking my head. Mallory has always been the easiest person to talk to. She's basically my mom and big sister, all wrapped up in one. I desperately want to tell her about Lora. Ask her for advice. But I'm not sure if she's going to freak out, because it's Lora, because she's Samantha's best friend, and because she's a decade older than me.

"Something else on your mind?" Mallory asks.

"God, how do you do that?" I ask, flopping back onto my bed. She flops down next to me.

"Sister powers," she says. "So, what is *actually* up? Is this moping about some app guy or something else?"

I think about it and realize I'm incredibly grateful she walked in before I could send my boob pic to Dan. He wasn't the most interesting guy. And he liked jazz music. And hated tacos. And his dick pic wasn't very impressive. And I consider myself pansexual and open to anyone, but...I think I like Lora's breasts, soft skin, and pretty eyes way more than Dan's dick. *Why was I even talking to Dan in the first place?*

"It's not Dan," I say quietly. "I kind of...hooked up with someone else. And then I kind of...maybe overreacted about something. And now I don't know what to do."

Mallory props herself up on an elbow. "You hooked up?"

I nod, feeling my face warm with a blush.

"Oh my god, Nelly!" Mallory squeals. "Was that your first time?"

I nod again.

"And it wasn't good?" Mallory asks quietly. "He didn't treat you right?"

"No, it was good," I say, and feel my blush deepen. "It's just...*she* wasn't there when I woke up, and it kind of freaked me out. Like it didn't mean the same thing to her as it did to me. But she says it did. So...maybe I overreacted. Maybe I'm an idiot. Maybe I'm being over emotional because it was my first time, and I was just so upset when I woke up and she wasn't there."

"Where was she?" Mallory asks. She already knows I'm pan, so she doesn't seem surprised that I was talking to Dan, but then ended up with a girl.

"Helping Mountain Rescue," I explain. "A tree fell and was blocking the road up the mountain."

"That seems like a noble thing to do," Mallory says. "Maybe she just didn't realize you'd be so upset about her not being there."

I nod. "She didn't."

"And do you like, really, really like her?" Mallory asks. "I mean, if she was worthy enough to be your first time and all, it must have been someone you were really into and trusted."

"Yes, all the above," I tell her. "I just...I think I've overreacted. I don't want to lose her."

"Who is it?" Mallory asks. "Please, tell me!"

I take a deep breath in and then let it all out. "Lora."

Mallory's jaw drops. And then she composes herself.

"Oh, Nelly," Mallory says. "I don't know how Samantha is going to feel about this..."

"How do *you* feel about it?" I ask.

"You said you really like her, and you said she treats you right, besides her minor mishap this morning," she says. "And it's Lora. We've all known her forever. She's a good person, everyone knows that. I might think she's a tiny bit older than you, and Samantha might be weirded out since it's her best friend...but I have met couples with bigger age gaps. Dad was twelve years older than mom, after all. If you're happy, then I want to be happy for you. I'll do my best to smooth things over with Samantha."

Chapter Twelve: Lora

I look up when I see the patio doors open, and my heart thuds in my chest when I see Mallory walking out, arm in arm with Nelly. Nelly looks stunning, wearing a white sundress and sandals, her blond hair flowing over her shoulders. Nelly untwines her arm from Mallory and makes a beeline for me, where I'm chatting with Levi and Jake and avoiding Samantha. It's hard to pull my eyes away from Nelly, but I notice Mallory head on over to Samantha, looking like a big sister on a mission.

"Lora?" Nelly says. "Can I talk to you? Alone?"

I glance at Levi and Jake, who both look a bit puzzled, especially when Nelly slips her hand into mine and leads me away from the other party guests. Silently, she walks me down a trail, the trees closing in around us, until we get to a little pond with a wooden bench. Nelly takes a seat and I sit next to her, giving her hand a squeeze.

She looks up at me, her big brown eyes looking open and tender.

"I'm sorry," Nelly says. "I'm sorry I overreacted about you leaving while I was sleeping and shut you out on the ride up here. I don't want to—"

Before she can finish, I slide my hand around her neck, cupping the back of her head, so I can pull her into a kiss. I make it tender and soft, and she moans, sending a sharp sensation of want right down to my core. I pull away, resting my forehead on hers.

"Nelly, you have nothing to apologize for," I tell her. "I wasn't thinking. I should have been there this morning. I should have held you in my arms until you woke up. I should have made love to you as the sun was rising. I promise you'll never wake up alone again for the rest of your life. I'll be there. Every single day of your life: I'll be there."

"Every day?" Nelly asks quietly. "Is that what you want?"

"Last night meant everything to me," I tell her. "I want you, all of you, to officially be mine. I want us to be together forever."

"I want all of that, too," she says and bites her lip. "But I kind of fell asleep after you gave me the most amazing orgasm of my life, and I never got to return the favor, so now I have to fix that."

"But what about Samantha?" I ask. "We should talk to her."

"Mallory is taking care of Samantha," Nelly says. "And I want to make you feel good, like you did to me."

"Here?" I ask, but she's already slipping off the bench and kneeling before me. She reaches up, undoing the fly of my jeans, pulling down the zip...

"No one is around," Nelly says softly.

I lift my hips and let her slide my jeans off, along with my underwear. She smiles up at me before leaning in, hesitantly licking up my slit. Then she moans, her lips and tongue finding my clit, followed by some exploration with her fingers. She pauses and I realize she's looking up at me.

"Why...are...you stopping?" I pant. I reach down, running my hand through her hair.

"It's good?" Nelly asks.

"So fucking good," I tell her.

She pushes herself up so she can kiss me on the lips, my taste on her tongue, before kneeling back down before me. She claims she's inexperienced, but my girl is about to win Rookie of the Year. I moan as she fingers me, her eyes intent on my pussy, watching her own fingers sink into me. I don't know why, but watching her intent focus on my pussy makes me even wetter. She pulls her sopping fingers out, circling my wetness on my aching clit. I move my hips into her touch, wanting so much more, but loving the fact that she's getting to know my body, taking it all in, seeming to note each moan and hitch of my breath as she applies more pressure to my clit, and then sinks her fingers back in.

Nelly's mouth returns to my clit, and I feel my orgasm build. She must feel it, too, because she changes from curious exploration to a woman on a mission to get me off. My body tenses up as the pleasure runs through me, and then I look down at her, smiling up at me, looking triumphant.

"Come here," I tell her, and she climbs into my lap and pulls me into a kiss.

Epilogue: One Year Later, Lora

My beautiful wife wakes up next to me, a dreamy look on her face as she reaches out, caressing my cheek. I take her hand in mine, kissing each of her knuckles.

"Good morning, Nelly," I tell her, just like I've done every morning for the past year. I run my hand down her body, coming to rest on her pussy, teasing her gently. But then I slide down further under the covers, positioning myself between her thighs, and slowly lick up her slit. I know she likes it soft and slow in the morning. I reach up and part her folds so I can dip my tongue in, tasting her sweetness, and I feel her grip on my hair tighten.

"Fuck...Lora..." Nelly moans.

I continue to taste her, to lap her up, to suck on her clit, until she's pulling my hair, begging for her release. But I pause, kissing my way up her body, her belly button and between her breasts, until I reach her mouth. I want to be kissing her when she comes. I reach back down, my fingers circling her clit, nice and slow, drawing her orgasm out of her as if we have all the time in the world. Because we do. This is our forever.

Gemma Addison Dove

Gemma (she/her) is a sapphic storyteller who enjoys writing steamy but sweet romance and spicy erotic romance.

If you liked this story, please consider following Gemma on
Instagram & TikTok @gemma.addison.dove
For more information about Gemma and to sign-up for her newsletter, please visit: gemmaaddisondove.com
(or payhip.com/gemmaaddisondove)

SUMMER LOVE

Samantha is a reclusive mountain woman, and that's just fine with her. But Samantha's sister, Mallory, drags the stoic mountain woman out of her cabin and forces her to attend Camp Pride's staff party. Samantha's old high school sweetheart has returned to the tiny mountain town to work at the summer camp as an art teacher. Sparks fly between Samantha and Caroline, their old flame quickly rekindling. But Caroline will only be in town for two months, so they agree to have a no strings attached summer fling. No one's ever had problems with that arrangement, right?

Summer Love is a steamy **sapphic** instalove short romance featuring a mountain woman and a cute art teacher finding true love. It is the second book in the *Sapphic Mountain Collection*, and while all of the stories are standalones, it is better to read them in order.

This quick read includes:

- Sapphic/Lesbian romance.

- Low angst instalove short romance.

- Sweet but steamy.

- Reunited high school sweethearts.

- Both characters are in their thirties.

- Mountain Woman + Art Teacher.

- Soft Butch + Femme.

- No strings attached summer fling.

- (or so they think)

- Can be read as a standalone.

College Dorm Girls, Volume One

College Dorm Girls: Volume One is a collection of the first four short stories in the College Dorm Girls Collection. Available on Amazon.

First Time: Angel is a heavy sleeper - she even sleeps through her roommate's early morning lovemaking sessions. Little does she know, they wish she'd wake up and join them...But when she does, they realize this will be Angel's first time. Hailee and Olivia are more than happy to guide their friend.

Just Dinner, Part One: College student Jenny has been invited to dinner at Senator Gloria Graham's mansion. Jenny is on the autism spectrum and is nervous about the formal dinner, so her roommate Martina tags along. Jenny is unexpectedly outed as pansexual during the dinner, but Martina helps her cope; and tells Jenny that she's pan, too. The roommates had no idea they had both been pining for each other, but now they're ready to make up for lost time.

Just Dinner, Part Two: Jenny and Martina first met Vera, the senator's daughter, at an awkward dinner party. Vera goes to their college, and ever since the dinner, they keep bumping into her. The three girls decide it must be fate, especially since they're all interested in being more than friends.

Birthday Girl: It's Harper's birthday, and her girlfriends, Ava and Millie, have a special evening planned. There's going to be cake, strawberries, whipped cream, and...handcuffs. And it's going to be Harper's best birthday ever.

This is a collection of spicy sapphic short stories intended for mature audiences.